W9-CDX-656

Welcome to

Hopscotch Hill School!

In Miss Sparks's class,

you will make friends

with children just like you.

They love school,

and they love to learn!

Keep an eye out for Razzi,

the class pet rabbit.

He may be anywhere!

See if you can spot him

as you read the story.

The Tooth Club!

Miss Sparks

New Member!

Hallie

Razzi

Logan

Skylar

Avery

Spencer

Nathan

Gwen

Lindy

Delaney

Connor

Published by Pleasant Company Publications
Copyright © 2004 by American Girl, LLC
All rights reserved. No part of this book may be used or reproduced
in any manner whatsoever without written permission except in the case
of brief quotations embodied in critical articles and reviews.
For information, address:
Book Editor, American Girl, 8400 Fairway Place,
P.O. Box 620998, Middleton, WI 53562.

Visit our Web site at **americangirl.com**

Printed in China
05 06 07 08 09 10 C&C 10 9 8 7 6

Hopscotch Hill School™ and logo, Hopscotch Hill™,
Where a love for learning grows™, Hallie™, and
American Girl® are trademarks of American Girl, LLC.

Cataloging-in-Publication data available from the Library of Congress

Teasing Trouble

by Valerie Tripp *illustrated by* Joy Allen

Giggles and Wiggles

One day Miss Sparks said,
"Good morning, boys and girls.
Who has news for our class today?"
Spencer shot his hand into the air.

Hallie raised her hand too.
Miss Sparks called on Spencer
because he raised his hand first.

Spencer said, "I have a new joke."

"Hurray!" cheered all the children.

Spencer said, "Knock, knock."

The children asked, "Who's there?"

Spencer said, "Who."

The children asked, "Who, who?"

Spencer asked, "Is there an owl in here?"

All the children laughed.

Miss Sparks laughed too.

The sparkles on her eyeglasses glittered.

The children hooted like owls.

"Who, who?" they hooted. "Who, who?"

Miss Sparks said, "All right, boys and girls.

Let's thank Spencer for his joke."

The children said, "Thank you, Spencer."

Spencer hooted, "Who, who?"

The children giggled.

"You! Thank you!" they said.

"That's who, who. Who, who!"

Hallie raised her hand again.

But the children were still hooting,

"Who, who! Who, who!"

Miss Sparks clapped her hands for quiet.

"Boys and girls," she said.

"Let's give Hallie our attention now."

Hallie said,"My two front teeth

are loose."

Spencer said, "Show us!"

Hallie wiggled her two front teeth.

"Oooh!" sighed all the children.

Hallie held up a little pillow

with a pocket on the back.

She said, "When my

teeth fall out,

I'll put them

in this pillow.

I'll hang it by my bed

for the tooth fairy."

Miss Sparks said,

"When your teeth fall out,

I will put your

picture in the

Tooth Club."

Hallie could not

wait to be in

the Tooth Club!

Connor said, "Wow!

Two loose teeth."

Logan said,

"And front teeth too."

Spencer said, "I wish I were

a two-loose-toother like Hallie.

And that's the tooth.

I mean, that's the truth."

Everyone laughed at Spencer's joke.

Gwen said, "Hallie, wiggle

your teeth again."

Hallie wiggled her teeth back and forth.

"Oooh!" sighed all the children.

Spencer jumped up.

"Look at me," he said.

"I have two loose ears."

Spencer wiggled his ears.

Everyone laughed.

Spencer grinned.

He loved to make

the children laugh!

At lunch Spencer said,

"Look, Hallie. Here's how

you should eat your sandwich."

Spencer held his sandwich

to the side of his mouth

like a flute.

Spencer used his side teeth

to bite into his sandwich.

Hallie giggled at Spencer.

She held her sandwich

to the side of her mouth.

She bit into her

sandwich with her side teeth.

Spencer said to Hallie,

"I have a tuna fish sandwich.

Do you have a tooth-a fish sandwich?"

Everyone laughed at Spencer's joke.

Nathan said, "Wiggle your teeth

for us, Hallie."

Hallie put down her sandwich.

She wiggled her two loose teeth.

"Oooh," sighed all the children.

"Do it again," said Avery.

Hallie wiggled

her two loose teeth again.

Spencer said, "Hallie, your teeth

are going to get tired.

You should hold them still and

wiggle yourself instead.

Look at me."

Spencer held his

two front teeth

and wiggled

the rest of his body.

Hallie giggled

and all the other children

laughed at funny Spencer.

Just then Hallie felt something

in her mouth.

She said, "Oh! My tooth!"

Hallie held up her tooth

so that everyone could see it.

"Oooh," sighed all the children.

Spencer stood up.

He clapped his hands for quiet,

just as Miss Sparks did.

Spencer said, "Boys and girls!

Let's give Hallie our attention now.

One of Hallie's loose teeth

has come out.

Hallie is in the Tooth Club."

"Hurray!" cheered all the children.

They clapped and cheered for Hallie.

Hallie smiled a big smile.

She was so glad

to be in the Tooth Club!

Spencer pretended

to be a cheerleader.

He waved his arms to make everyone

cheer louder for Hallie.

Everyone laughed and cheered louder.

Spencer smiled a big smile.

He was so glad

to make his friends laugh!

Two-Tooth To-Do

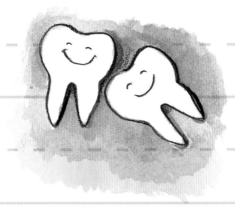

After lunch the children went outside.

Spencer said, "Let's play Hopscotch."

But no one paid attention to Spencer.

All the children stood around Hallie.

Avery asked Hallie,

"May I see your tooth?"

Hallie said, "Yes."

Nathan asked, "May I see it after Avery?"

Hallie said, "Yes."

Gwen and Skylar said,

"We want to see the tooth too!"

Spencer wanted everyone's attention.

He shouted, "Look, everybody!

I'm Hallie pulling out her tooth."

Everyone looked at Spencer.

Spencer pretended to yank out

his tooth with two hands.

Everyone laughed.

Spencer felt better.

He pretended to yank out

his tooth again.

He yowled. He pretended

to wave his tooth around.

All the children

watched funny Spencer.

Just then Hallie felt something in her mouth.

She said, "Oh! My tooth!"

Her second tooth had come out!

"Hurray!" cheered all the children.

Hallie smiled.

There was a big space in her mouth

where her two front teeth used to be.

Spencer shouted, "Hey, everybody!

Hallie has a hole in her head!"

Some children laughed.

Hallie frowned.

This time she did not like Spencer's joke.

Spencer did not notice.

He was laughing too hard.

Gwen said, "Spencer, I think your jokes

are starting to hurt Hallie's feelings."

Spencer said, "Hallie doesn't mind.

You have a hole in your head too, Gwen.

It's your nose!"

A few children laughed.

Gwen did not laugh.

She rolled her eyes.

She walked away from Spencer.

Spencer started to sing,

"Hallie has a hole in her head,

Hallie has a hole in her head."

Only a very few children laughed.

Spencer thought maybe

the other children did not hear him.

So Spencer sang louder.

Hallie blushed angrily.

She wished Spencer would stop.

But Spencer sang his song louder,

and louder, and louder.

He wanted to make all the children laugh.

When the class went inside,

Hallie showed Miss Sparks

the two teeth that had fallen out.

Then Hallie put her teeth

in the pocket of the pillow.

Miss Sparks put Hallie's picture

in the Tooth Club.

Miss Sparks said, "I will put two stars

next to your picture, Hallie.

That way we will remember

that you lost two front teeth

on the same day."

Everyone clapped and cheered for Hallie.

Spencer thought that they were making

a big fuss and to-do over Hallie's teeth.

A big two-tooth to-do!

Spencer followed Hallie to the art table.

Hallie drew a picture of a fairy.

She glued it to her tooth pillow.

Hallie said, "Now the tooth fairy

will be sure to find my teeth."

All the children at the art table smiled.

Everyone knew that

Hallie loved fairies.

Spencer joked, "Uh-oh, Hallie.

The tooth fairy is going to be mad at you.

The tooth fairy isn't strong enough

to fly with two teeth."

Hallie's face changed from happy to sad.

The children at the art table frowned.

This time they did not think

Spencer was so funny.

Skylar said, "You should not tease Hallie

about the tooth fairy, Spencer."

Spencer said, "There's no such thing

as the tooth fairy anyway.

Only babies believe in the tooth fairy."

All the children at the art table gasped.

They were shocked at Spencer

for saying such a mean thing.

Hallie decided to ignore Spencer.

She turned her back to him.

She showed her pillow to Skylar.

Hallie said, "See, Skylar?"

But Hallie had no front teeth.

So it sounded as if she said,

"Th-ee, Th-kylar?"

Spencer laughed.

Spencer said, "Hey, everybody!

Listen to Hallie. She talks funny!"

Now Hallie felt angry.

Her face was red.

She walked away from Spencer.

But Spencer did not notice.

He followed Hallie.

He imitated the way Hallie talked.

He said, "I th-ee, Hallie."

Spencer laughed and laughed.

He laughed so much that

he did not notice that

no one else was laughing.

This time no one thought

that Spencer was funny at all.

Funny and Nice

At the end of the day

the children lined up to go home.

Hallie held her tooth pillow.

Spencer stood behind Hallie.

Miss Sparks said, "Oh, Hallie!

Your pillow is beautiful."

Hallie said, "Thanks, Miss Sparks."

Miss Sparks moved away.

Spencer imitated Hallie.

He whispered, "Thank-th, Mi-th Th-park-th!"

Hallie whirled around fast.

"Stop it, Spencer!" she said in a strong voice.

But Spencer imitated Hallie again.

He said, "Th-top it, Th-pen-ther!"

Hallie stamped her foot.

Her face was red and angry.

Hallie said, "Spencer, I am tired of your teasing. You are a big, mean bully!"

Spencer was shocked.

He felt terrible.

He had never meant to make Hallie angry.

Spencer wished that he could think of something funny to say.

But he could not.

Suddenly, Spencer didn't feel funny at all.

Miss Sparks hurried over.

The sparkles on her eyeglasses

were not glittering.

Miss Sparks said, "Spencer and Hallie,

I would like to speak to you."

All the other children left.

Miss Sparks said to Hallie and Spencer,

"Please tell me what happened."

Hallie said, "Spencer has been acting

like a bully."

Spencer said, "I'm not a bully!

A bully picks on littler people

and pinches and punches them."

Hallie said to Spencer, "You didn't

hurt me by pinching or punching.

But your words hurt my feelings."

Spencer said sadly, "I didn't mean to.

I was only joking."

Hallie said, "Your jokes were funny at first.

But then you started to make fun of me,

and you would not stop."

Spencer hung his head sadly.

Miss Sparks said, "Hallie, did you try

to tell Spencer how you were feeling?"

Hallie shook her head no.

Miss Sparks put one hand

on Spencer's shoulder

and the other hand

on Hallie's shoulder.

Miss Sparks said kindly,

"Tell me something that each of you

will do differently from now on."

Spencer and Hallie were quiet.

Then Spencer said, "From now on,

I'll stop and think before I joke."

And Hallie said, "From now on,

I will speak up right away

when someone hurts my feelings."

Miss Sparks said,

"I am proud of both of you.

You have learned that

words can hurt and words can help."

Spencer said, "I sure wish I could
think of some words that would
help Hallie feel better."

Miss Sparks said, "I know you can.
You can be funny, Spencer.
I know that you can also be nice."

When Hallie came to school
the next day,
Spencer was waiting at her desk.
All the boys and girls watched them.

Spencer said, "I am sorry, Hallie.
I didn't stop to think about how
my jokes might make you feel.
I should not have teased you
about how you look
or how you talk.

I should not have said

that only babies believe

in the tooth fairy."

Spencer turned around.

All the boys and girls laughed.

Hallie laughed loudest of all.

Spencer was wearing the wings

from the dress-up closet!

Spencer had a sign on his back

that said, "Tooth Fairy's Helper."

He looked so silly!

He was making fun of himself

to apologize to Hallie.

Spencer said, "Knock, knock."

Hallie asked, "Who's there?"

Spencer said, "To."

Hallie asked, "To who?"

Spencer said, "To you. I want to

give this toothbrush to you."

Spencer gave Hallie a toothbrush

with a big pink bow on it.

Hallie smiled a big, wide smile.

She was not angry

at Spencer anymore.

Funny and Nice

Hallie said, "Thank you, Spencer.

I am sorry I called you a bully.

You are funny. And you are nice too."

"Thanks!" said Spencer.

He was so happy that

he fluttered his wings.

It was nice to be funny,

but it was nicer to be nice.

Spencer decided that from now on

he would be funny and nice Spencer.

Dear Parents . . .

Is your child like Spencer, who loves to make jokes but doesn't quite know when to stop? Or is she like Hallie, who doesn't speak up soon enough when her feelings are hurt? If she's like most children who are just starting school, she's a bit like *both* characters at one time or another. Children love to laugh and to make their friends laugh, too. But humor is tricky. What tickles one child's funny bone can hurt another's, and joking stings like teasing if your child lets it go too far before saying, "Stop!"

How can you help your child to be both nice and funny, considerate and comical, kindhearted and lighthearted? How can you teach her to stand up for herself against teasing? Try some of the following activities, suggested by the Hopscotch Hill School advisory board. The activities will help your child grow in empathy, compassion, and confidence as she learns to read others' feelings and express her own.

Kind & Considerate

Your child comes at the world with her arms and her heart wide open. She wants to be kind, loving, and considerate of other people, but she hasn't quite learned how to tell what others are feeling or how to help them feel better. Thoughtfulness is a learned skill, and one that you can teach your child to value in herself and in others.

• Play **Read My Face.** Make different facial expressions, and ask your child to name the emotions you're showing. Let her make faces, too, and see if you can name the emotions. Together, look at the illustrations in *Teasing Trouble,* and ask your child how Hallie's expression changes from one illustration to another. What are some clues that she is feeling excited and proud, hurt and unhappy, frustrated and angry, and then happy again?

• Model thoughtfulness. When you're collecting clothes for a shelter or preparing a food basket for an elderly friend or neighbor, **invite your child** to help. She can choose too-small clothes from her closet or help you make cookies to put in the basket. When you deliver the basket, bring your child along so that she can see how her contributions make another person feel.

• Give your child chances to care for others, such as a dog or a younger sibling. **Praise her** with specific words, such as, "You're brushing Sam's fur so gently. See his tail wagging? You're making him happy!" Ask your child how her act of kindness makes her feel, too.

• Care for your child **out loud.** While you're nursing an injury or wiping away her tears, express empathy by telling her that you can imagine how she feels. Express sympathy by telling her that you are sad that she is sad. As you comfort her, express love and kindness by telling her how good it feels to be able to help her feel better. You'll give her words to use when she cares for someone else who needs comforting.

Wise Wit or Wisecrack?

Joking, clowning, and acting just plain silly come naturally to children. It's not called "kidding around" for nothing! But children don't always know the difference between making something fun and funny and making fun, which *isn't* funny. How can you help your child use her wit wisely?

- Talk with your child about when jokes are okay and when they're not okay. Help her tease out the difference between laughing *with* others, which is good humor, and laughing *at* others, which is bad humor. **Wiggle your ears,** and then wiggle her ears to remind her that words that sound funny to one person can sound like a put-down to someone else.

- As you read *Teasing Trouble*, pretend there is a **"pause button"** that you or your child can hit when either of you wants to stop and talk about the story.

Ask your child to tell you when she thinks Spencer's joking begins to feel like teasing to Hallie. Talk about how joking can get out of hand.

- Model gentle, **wise wit instead of wisecracks** for your child. Try to be aware of and beware of making jokes about someone else's appearance, actions, or speech. Remember that the child sitting beside you on the couch is watching you more closely than she's watching that television sitcom. Take the opportunity to talk with her about what you're both seeing and hearing and to help her distinguish good humor from bad.

- Encourage your child to tell jokes or riddles that will make you both laugh and feel great. Then talk to her about **other things she does** that feel good, such as inviting someone to play or giving someone a compliment, sympathy, or help. Encourage these other ways of making friends and getting attention, too.

- If your child needs to apologize to a friend, talk about different ways to **say she's sorry.** Help her use her talents and strengths, such as drawing a picture for her friend or using her sense of humor to make things better, as Spencer does. If she has butterflies in her stomach before the apology, reassure her that though apologizing isn't easy, she'll feel better afterward—and her friend will, too.

That's Not Funny!

All children face mean-spirited words and bullying at one time or another. You can help your child have the confidence to stand up, speak out, and say "Stop!" When she does so with words and actions that are polite and powerful, she'll be helping other children learn that their unkind words are not okay.

- Teach your child **three steps** for dealing with words or actions that she does not like: (1) She should count to five before saying anything back—especially something mean. (2) She should look the other child in the eye and say, "Please stop!" in a strong voice. (3) She should walk away.

- Help your child practice using **"I" messages,** such as "I feel angry when you call me 'four eyes.' Stop it." Role-play with your child or use dolls or puppets until she is comfortable saying those words in a strong voice. Reread *Teasing Trouble,* and brainstorm with your child some things Hallie could have said when Spencer's jokes began to feel like bullying to her.

- **"Ask three before me."** Encourage your child to ask the other child three times to stop before she asks you or a teacher to step in. That will give her a chance to use and build her own skills to resolve issues. If she does come to you for help, ask her, "How can I help you deal with that?" so that you can brainstorm solutions together.

- Toss a **ping-pong ball** playfully toward your daughter, and show her how it bounces off. Ask her to imagine harsh words or teasing bouncing off her, too. Tell her that she doesn't have to "catch" and keep a put-down. She can let it bounce right back to the teaser.

- Encourage your child to spend time with children who make her feel good, not bad. Talk with her about how she can **stand up for friends** who are being picked on, just as Gwen does for Hallie. And remind her that sometimes kids who bother others just want to play, too. Ask your child what she thinks would happen if she invited "the teaser" to play with her. Might she make a new friend?

This story and the "Dear Parents" activities were developed with guidance from the Hopscotch Hill School advisory board:

Dominic Gullo is a professor of Early Childhood Education at Queens College, City University of New York. He is a member of the governing board of the National Association for the Education of Young Children, and he is a consultant to school districts across the country in the areas of early childhood education, curriculum, and assessment.

Margaret Jensen has taught beginning reading for 32 years and is currently a math resource teacher in the Madison Metropolitan School District, Wisconsin. She has served on committees for the International Reading Association and the Wisconsin State Reading Association, and has been president of the Madison Area Reading Council. She has presented at workshops and conferences in the areas of reading, writing, and children's literature.

Kim Miller is a school psychologist at Stephens Elementary in Madison, Wisconsin, where she works with children, parents, and teachers to help solve—and prevent—problems related to learning and adjustment to the classroom setting.

Virginia Pickerell has worked with teachers and parents as an educational consultant and counselor within the Madison Metropolitan School District. She has researched and presented workshops on topics such as learning processes, problem solving, and creativity. She is also a former director of Head Start.